BIOLOOD

Titles in Papercuts:

THE TRICK
KATE ORMAND

DARK TIDE
JON MAYHEW

SCISSOR MAN
TIM COLLINS

ONE WAY
KATE ORMAND

QUEEN OF FLIES
TIM COLLINS

WAXWORK
TIM COLLINS

ALICE
DANNY PEARSON

THE LANE
IAIN MCLAUGHLIN

THE SICKNESS
JACQUELINE RAYNER

WANTED
JENNI SPANGLER

A LITTLE SECRET
ANN EVANS

BIOLOGY
EMMA NORRY

Badger Publishing Limited, Oldmedow Road, Hardwick Industrial Estate, King's Lynn PE30 4JJ

Telephone: 01438 791037

www.badgerlearning.co.uk

BIOLOGY

EMMA NORRY | MARK PENMAN

*"Remember: if you've got nothing nice to say,
don't say anything at all."*

Biology ISBN 978-1-78837-384-5

Text © Emma Norry 2019
Complete work © Badger Publishing Limited 2019

Publisher / Senior Editor: Danny Pearson
Editor: Claire Morgan
Copyeditor: Cheryl Lanyon
Designer: Bigtop Design Ltd
Illustration: Mark Penman

2 4 6 8 10 9 7 5 3 1

CHAPTER 1

THE SKELETON

Samir scanned his biology classroom. It had been repainted since last term. There was no teacher yet — a rarity at Wallace Academy. Usually teachers were waiting. Making sure no one was too rowdy, especially on the first day of a new term.

"Yo, losers!" Samir yelled. His best friends Akim and Rasheed had walked in.

Samir had only seen them once over the summer.

"Hey, man!" Akim high-fived Samir, and Rasheed fist-bumped him. As more students came into the classroom, the noise levels rose.

"How was your summer?" Samir asked, leaning on a desk.

"I can't believe it's over and that we're back at this dump already," Rasheed moaned.

"I know," Akim said. "Glad we're in the same biology class, though."

"Maybe we'll get to see more pictures of naked bodies this term?" Samir cracked up.

The bell had already rung, but with no sign of Mr Bones, and his mates egging him on, Samir walked up to the full-length model skeleton next to the whiteboard. It stood limply, with its head drooping. He shook its hand. "Lovely to meet you. You're new around here, aren't you? I'm Samir."

Katie, who quite liked Samir when he wasn't being over the top, yelled from the back, "Ooh Samir, got yourself a new girlfriend?"

"Well at least this one won't talk too much," Samir joked.

"Ha, ha!" She threw a pencil in his direction.

Samir perched on the empty teacher's desk, pushing aside the model mini-torso. He offered a half-eaten chocolate bar to the skeleton. "Hungry?"

A few kids laughed and, as usual, Samir had to take it further. He stood up and pretended to leer at the skeleton. "Let's arrange some alone time," he said, raising an eyebrow. "Old stinky-Bones isn't here yet!" Samir slunk his arm around the skeleton's waist and tried to pull it closer. As he did, he pulled a face as if he was going to be sick. "Eww, this thing stinks!"

Rasheed gave a warning cough and only then did Samir notice that the laughter had died down. He stopped grinning.

A tall, pale man, dressed in a white lab coat,

stood behind him. "I'm Mr Medon, your new biology teacher," he rasped. It sounded as if he was a heavy smoker and had a sore throat at the same time.

Samir sized him up. This man was as skinny as a garden rake and didn't look old enough to be out of college. First teaching job, Samir reckoned. They could all have a right laugh. He probably didn't have a clue.

"Hello, Sir." Samir straightened up, adjusting his tie.

"Where's old Bones?" Akim piped up.

Mr Medon didn't reply. He stood behind his desk and slowly touched the heart inside the model torso.

Then he stepped forwards, uncomfortably close to Samir. Bending towards him, Mr Medon smiled broadly, right in Samir's face. His lips stretched so wide that Samir thought his face might crack. Medon's lips parted and Samir found himself staring at a row of uneven, yellow teeth.

Mr Medon jerked back and waved Samir away curtly. "Go to your seat, boy. Mr Bones will not be returning to Wallace High."

Murmurs about Mr Bones flew around the classroom as Samir headed back to his seat.

"Quiet!" Mr Medon barked. "Open your textbooks to Chapter 6. Today we'll be looking at medicine from ancient times. In particular — the use of leeches."

Pages were quickly turned.

Samir whispered to Akim and Rasheed, "Bet *he'd* suck your blood!"

At the front of the class, Mr Medon put his hand on the back of the skeleton's head and lifted it, leaning in as if listening carefully. When he took his hand away, the head didn't droop down again, but stayed exactly in place, as if staring at them all. Medon coughed and swallowed hard, straining his neck forwards.

"Class! I want you to treat this skeleton with respect. Once, he too was a living, breathing creature, just like you all are now. This is no plastic model. In fact, I helped pick the flesh off his bones myself." He smirked.

Staring at the skeleton, Samir shuddered. Had he just touched real human bones? No way! But the longer he looked at the skull now, the less sure he was that he could trust his own eyes. Did those teeth just move? He could have sworn he saw them bite down.

The class laughed nervously. They looked around at each other. This new teacher wasn't funny. He was weird. Unpredictable — the worst kind.

Mr Medon glided towards Samir's desk, pointing his bony finger towards Samir's chest.

Medon's nails were long, pointed and dirty. "The way you just behaved with my bony friend was… inappropriate."

Samir flinched at the teacher's breath. It reminded him of that time he'd found a dead cat by the side of the road.

"Sorry, Sir. I was only messing. I didn't mean any harm."

"No harm, hmm?" Mr Medon replied. "Well. We'll see what Mr Skeleton thinks about that, shall we? You should only say nice things to people, Samir." Medon folded his hands together, bony fingers overlapping. He cracked his knuckles.

Samir shifted in his seat, but then forced a smirk. "Don't think it can hear much of what anyone says… *Sir*."

"Right," Mr Medon clapped his hands together, "detention for you." His eyes fluttered closed for a moment, like he was about to pray. "Come back here at lunchtime. We'll see how much of your time I can waste since you are so good at wasting other people's."

As soon as Mr Medon's back was turned, Samir rolled his eyes.

Mr Medon's voice was smooth and cold. "I knew you'd be an eye-roller, Samir. I can always tell. Eye-rollers, face-pullers, predictable boys with their rude finger gestures." He hissed. "I've seen them all before. I'd be careful if I were you..."

CHAPTER 2
HEART AND LUNGS

Samir and his friends walked down the corridor.

"Can't believe mean Medon gave you a detention!" Rasheed said. "That means Akim will have to go in goal."

Samir slapped Akim on the back, saying, "And you're a rubbish goalie, mate!"

"I'm not!" Akim punched Samir in the arm.

"After lunch, wait for me by my locker, yeah?" Samir said.

Samir entered the biology classroom just minutes after the lunch bell rang. Mr Medon smiled grimly as he walked in. "Hello again, Samir."

"I prefer Sammy."

"I don't," Mr Medon said. "Take a seat."

Samir moved towards the back of the class but Mr Medon said sharply, "No. Sit up here. In front of my desk, so I can keep my eye on you."

Samir took a seat. The classroom looked different, empty of his friends. He hoped Akim wasn't going to let too many goals in.

The skeleton had been moved, its hands now taped to its hips, as if about to tell someone off. The room was colder than earlier, too. Much colder, even though it was only September. And the heating had usually been turned on by now. Samir pulled his blazer closer around him.

Samir put his lunchbox on his desk. He was about to open his bottle of apple juice when Mr Medon said abruptly, "I don't think so. Eat in your own time. This isn't a cafeteria."

"But I'm thirsty, Sir," Samir pleaded.

Medon didn't look up from a book he was reading. "You won't die. You can wait."

Samir stuffed his lunchbox back into his bag. Could Mr Medon even do that? Wasn't it illegal to stop him from drinking?

"So," Mr Medon murmured, "let's see how much biology you actually know. But first, tell me — what body part do you value most?"

Samir stared at him and almost cracked a smile. If his mates were here he'd come up with the perfect joke. But his mates weren't here. And this new teacher seemed to have it in for him.

"My brain, I suppose. It's kind of useful, right?" He hoped a little humour might soften Medon up a bit. Maybe he'd show a more… human side, one-on-one.

"Judging by the joking around you're so fond of, I'd guess you quite value your mouth?"

Samir shrugged. "That too, I guess."

Mr Medon clasped his hands together and rested his bony chin on top. "You should spend less time guessing. If you'd engaged your brain earlier, then you might not be here now. But, here we are."

Samir noticed how strange Mr Medon's eyes were. Almond-shaped, and instead of the pupil being round and black, it was like a cat's eye, almost a vertical slit. They hadn't looked like that earlier, Samir was sure.

"What are your lungs for?" Mr Medon asked.

Samir swallowed. "Lungs? To breathe, Sir."

"Can you live with only one?"

Samir had no idea.

Mr Medon smiled. "Take a nice deep breath. Right now."

Samir did as he was told.

"Note how that feels. You don't smoke, or have any… breathing difficulties, do you?"

Samir shook his head. He breathed in deeply through his nose again. His chest expanded. He held the breath for a second before letting it out.

"Calming isn't it?" said Medon. "Now, imagine not being able to do that. Breathe. Wouldn't that be… terrible?"

Samir nodded, his stomach suddenly twisting. He needed the toilet. "It would, Sir. Awful." Samir tried to make his voice sincere, aware of how intense Mr Medon sounded.

"Indeed. If you were punched or kicked hard enough, you wouldn't be able to breathe properly or run then, would you?"

"No, Sir."

"Now, draw me a picture of the lungs. Make sure you label the parts clearly." He handed Samir a piece of plain paper but, as Samir grabbed it, Mr Medon yanked it sharply back.

"Ow!" Samir yelled. He stared at the paper cut running up his thumb and frowned as the blood swelled.

"Oh, sorry," Mr Medon said, turning away and not sounding sorry at all. It sounded more like he was smiling. "Just a paper cut, isn't it? Surface wound. Nothing major. Nothing… lasting."

Yes, it was just a paper cut. Not deep, but it still stung. Samir sucked his thumb and then quickly took it out of his mouth. He smoothed out the paper in front of him. One corner had almost an entire smeared thumbprint of blood. Samir drew in silence, carefully labelling the trachea and bronchi.

"Could we open a window, Sir? It's very hot." It had been freezing a moment ago. Was Mr Medon messing with the heating as some sort of punishment?

Mr Medon's raspy voice cut through the quiet, stuffy classroom. "What do you think having no heart would mean?" he asked.

Samir felt irritated. "Um… you'd be dead."

"I don't just mean the reality. I mean, imagine living with no… feelings. No emotions. Unable to love or care about… anything. Hearts are complicated. Then again, we're all complicated inside, aren't we?"

"Riiii-ght," Samir said slowly. He shook his head and carried on drawing. This man had lost it, clearly. Already the pressure of teaching must have got to him.

"I used to go to this school myself." Mr Medon's voice had grown quieter, and he sounded much younger. Did Samir hear a lisp? "I had old Bones for biology too." It was almost as if he was talking to himself. "He had it in for me."

This was the first interesting thing he'd said. Samir glanced up at him. "But you came back to teach?"

Mr Medon snapped, "Less talking — more drawing. After that lung, I need a diagram of your heart... I mean, a heart."

Samir blinked. Had Medon's eyes changed again? They'd looked oddly milky a second ago. Medon was obviously going to make biology a nightmare. Maybe he was being extra strict to prove himself, trying to get some respect.

It wasn't fair. It was only the first day of term and Samir had already missed lunch to spend time with this creep. He drew in silence.

Medon tapped his fingernails on a desk and the noise made Samir flinch. "You seem to have many friends, Samir."

Samir looked up. Medon was now standing over by the window and staring across the school yard.

Samir wanted to be out there playing football. He gritted his teeth, turned the piece of paper over and drew a heart as quickly as he could. Mr Medon probably wasn't even going to look at it.

The bell went for the end of lunchtime. Mr Medon didn't turn round from the window. His nose was almost pressed up against it. He said icily, "Go. Leave your paper on my desk."

Samir put his paper on Mr Medon's desk. He swung his bag over his shoulder, knocking the model torso onto the floor. Samir froze, but it was as if Mr Medon hadn't heard. Samir bent quickly to pick up the fallen parts. When his fingers fumbled to put the pieces back into the right places, he jammed an eyeball, a kidney and the heart into his trouser pocket. He left the room as fast as he could.

Once outside, Samir took the eyeball out of his pocket. He held it in his hand. He didn't know why he'd taken it — just keen to get away, probably. The eyeball reminded him of a snooker ball. Smooth.

*

Katie, Akim and Rasheed were waiting by his locker, all holding piles of books. Samir leaned towards Katie and sniffed. "You smell of chips and I'm starving!"

She pushed him away. "Get off! Was it awful?"

"Yeah. Medon's mad — nearly gave me a heart attack!" He clutched his heart.

Samir rolled the eyeball he was still holding around in his fingers.

"What's that?" Katie asked, nodding at it.

Samir laughed and closed one eye. "My eye fell out staring at Medon's ugly face for a whole hour."

"Don't be mean!" Katie whacked him on the arm.

Samir said, "It's a fact. And his breath stinks!"

"How do you know?" Rasheed said. He pulled on Samir's collar and breathed heavily down it. "Did he breathe down your neck while you ate your sandwiches?"

Samir sighed. "He wouldn't let me eat my lunch. He's trying to be tough. He hasn't got much going for him — skinnier than his skeleton friend. He was at school here, you know. Bet he got bullied. And now he's one of those miserable teachers who wants everyone else to be miserable too."

Mr Medon rounded the corner, just in time to see the four of them stroll away down the corridor.

"Oh Samir," he murmured, behind their backs. "Miserable? I haven't even started, my friend… you have no idea what I can do."

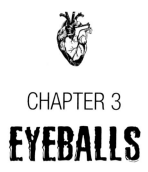

CHAPTER 3
EYEBALLS

In woodwork, Samir was gluing together a picture frame. He enjoyed woodwork. Mrs Burns liked to sit at the back reading her newspaper and just let everyone get on with it.

Katie drew little hearts in the corner of her frame.

"Ugh," Samir said, "that's a bit cheesy."

She frowned at him. "Don't you like it?"

"It looks great — if you're five years old!" he said, and sniggered. "Akim, what's up with yours?" He pointed to the glue dripping between the joints. "Looks like a five-year-old made that too!"

Akim shrugged. "I dunno. Keeps falling apart."

"Like your footballing skills, mate!"

"Whatever."

Rasheed held up his frame for Akim to see, but suddenly there was a gust of wind and the classroom door slammed shut with a crash. Rasheed jumped and the frame he was holding smashed right into Akim's face.

"Jeez!" Akim howled and clutched his face. "Something went in my eye!"

Samir saw a stream of blood flow down Akim's face and his stomach turned.

Akim fell to his knees. "I can't see!"

Katie and Rasheed crowded round him. "Akim's hurt!" Katie shouted. "Mrs Burns!"

Akim rocked back and forth, whimpering.

Mrs Burns rushed forwards, looking pale. "Step back, everyone!" she commanded. "Behave yourselves! Just sit here quietly until the bell goes."

She helped Akim up, put her arm round his shoulder and guided him out of the classroom.

Katie said, "What if some wood went into his eye? He might be blinded."

"Don't be such a drama queen!" Samir replied.

Rasheed frowned at him. "There was loads of blood, did you see it?"

"He'll find playing football even harder now, then!" Samir laughed and tried to high-five Rasheed.

Rasheed turned away. "Mate, not funny."

Katie stalked off.

"You've upset her, too," Rasheed said.

"I was just joking!" Samir cried.

Rasheed tutted. "You always go too far, man."

*

As they walked to biology, Samir tried to grab Katie's arm, but she shrugged him off.

Mr Medon sat at his desk, looking over a small, black book. As Samir approached, Mr Medon pushed the book aside. He peered over the top of his glasses. "Why are you late?"

"Um, there was a… situation in our last lesson, Sir."

"Yes, I'm aware of the unfortunate accident, Samir. Still, it didn't happen to *you*, did it?"

How did Medon know about Akim already?

Rasheed said, "Sorry, Sir. We had to take Akim's things down to the office."

Mr Medon didn't seem concerned about Akim; he gave Samir a slow, strange smile. He stood and clapped his hands. Samir noticed that his fingernails were even longer than they'd been yesterday. Quarter of an inch longer.

Rasheed nudged Samir when he sat down next to him. "Have you seen his nails? Maybe he needs them to pick that big beak of his!"

"He's like a witch!" Samir whispered.

"I have a treat for you today," Mr Medon announced. He placed both palms on his desk and flexed his long, bony fingers. The sound of his nails against the wood made Samir shudder. "We're lucky enough to have some eyeballs to dissect!" He gave one of his wide smiles, showing his yellow teeth. It gave Samir the creeps.

Katie raised her hand.

"Yes, Katie?"

"Sir, a splinter went into Akim's eye. I'm *really* not sure I can handle cutting up an eyeball today."

"Exactly why you should see an eyeball close up. See how it works and how it responds to being damaged. People get hurt every day, unfortunately, but the Earth still spins."

Over in the corner, Mr Medon opened a small refrigerator. He brought out a set of trays. Each one contained an eyeball, sitting in milky jelly.

"Now, stage one is to remove the connective tissue to produce a neatly trimmed eyeball. Leave the eyeball itself and the optic nerve rear cord intact," Mr Medon said clearly. He walked around the classroom and placed trays on the desks.

The noise levels rose as students squabbled over partners.

"Quieten down! Work in pairs. You lot, a three. Do not mess around with the scalpels!"

Samir, Rasheed and Katie, all stood at the same work station, stared at the tray in front of them. Katie made a sick face and Rasheed shook his head. "Gross."

Samir offered, "Come on, it won't be too bad. I'll do the cutting. One of you keep it steady." He sawed back and forth into the eyeball with a scalpel, while Katie gripped it with forceps. Rasheed flipped through his textbook to the page with the drawing of an eyeball.

Mr Medon called out instructions, weaving through the class and smiling at their repulsed faces. "When you make the first cut into the cornea, you may notice a runny, watery juice leaking out. It may be clear, or it may be dirty. This is the 'aqueous humour'."

"Very funny!" Rasheed said.

Samir replied, "Not for the poor sheep this has come from." He pressed down with the scalpel, but the eyeball was tough. He had to jab it in until he heard a 'pop'.

"Samir, you have something correct — for once," Mr Medon called across the classroom. "These are indeed sheep eyeballs!"

Suddenly, Katie screamed as liquid shot out of the eyeball. She wiped at her mouth furiously. "Eww! That goo!" She tried to spit, white foam dribbled down her chin and she ran out of the classroom.

Samir pulled a face. "Doesn't seem like eyeballs are very tasty!"

Rasheed laughed.

*

At home, Samir rushed up to his room and

flicked his television on. He had an hour of gaming before he had to finish his homework. He, Akim and Rasheed usually played FIFA together.

He texted Katie and then Akim the same message:

Hope you're OK.

Then he went onto Instant Messenger with Rasheed.

Samir: *Heard from Akim?*

Rasheed: *A splinter in his eye. His mum is going nuts! She's going to get woodwork closed down.*

Samir: *For real?*

Rasheed: *You know how stressed his mum gets. He can't see. Might need an operation.*

Samir: *Maybe he'll get an eye-patch?*

Rasheed: *Be serious, Samir!*

Samir: *Sorry. Just messing.*

Rasheed: *Can't believe Medon made us chop up eyeballs. Grim.*

Samir: *He enjoyed everyone being grossed out.*

Samir and Rasheed played a few FIFA games, then Rasheed said he needed to go offline.

Samir: *Need to wee again?*

Rasheed: *No joke, man.*

Samir: *You keep running off. Looking up cheat codes?*

Rasheed: *I'm in pain… my feet have gone all puffy. They've swelled up!*

Samir: *All those burgers you keep eating!*

Rasheed: *I just don't feel so good.*

Samir: *Because you're losing four-nil? Oh, come on!*

Rasheed: *No. Serious. My back is killing me! I'm going to log off. I'm really tired. Can't keep my eyes open.*

CHAPTER 4
BODY PARTS

Samir couldn't sleep. The last few days at school hadn't been much fun. That new teacher was so weird. Why did he have it in for him?

He checked his phone. Katie hadn't replied to any of his texts. He shouldn't have made so many jokes, but she knew what he was like! She usually enjoyed his sense of humour. He sent her another message, adding three smiley faces.

Rasheed hadn't stayed online long either. Maybe Samir had gone too far with his jokes.

Just as Samir felt himself dropping off, an image of the model torso on Mr Medon's desk flashed into his mind. He'd taken those body parts and stashed them in his locker. But they didn't belong to him, did they?

One of the parts was an eyeball. Akim had got a splinter in his eye.

Samir tried to remember what else he'd taken... a kidney, he'd stolen a kidney.

And now… two of his friends were in a bad way! One hurt and another ill in less than 24 hours. It was coincidence though, wasn't it?

What had Rasheed said earlier?

Samir Googled Rasheed's symptoms: going to the toilet a lot, back pain. The first thing that came up was 'kidney infection'.

But maybe Rasheed just had an upset stomach. That could easily be it. Samir hadn't taken the intestines, had he? Although the model intestines were just a painted block of plastic, the idea of intestines had always creeped him out. They were like a long, wet rope.

What was the other thing he'd taken?

Oh God, it was a heart!

He remembered what Medon had asked about lungs in detention. It was possible to exist with only one lung, or kidney, or eyeball, but you certainly couldn't live without a heart. Samir's own heart started to beat faster and faster.

Lying in his warm bed, he felt himself heat up under the sheets. He put his hand on his chest and felt his heart hammering. Medon had asked him what body parts he valued. Samir had said his brain. Was he getting a headache? He drank from the glass of water he kept on his bedside table. He was being silly. His mum always said he had an overactive imagination.

Medon had mentioned Samir's mouth. Samir swallowed. Was his throat sore now? Did his tongue feel like it was swelling? His heart galloped in his chest. He tried to slow down his breathing, but he could still hear the rush of blood in his ears.

Samir rubbed his eyes; they were stinging. He couldn't sleep. He got up and sat at his desk. He opened his biology textbook and flipped to the section on the heart. He stared at the words and diagrams. The heart had chambers and muscles and blood vessels.

Samir stretched across his desk to reach his phone. He should text his friends, but what would he say? It would just sound like a joke. It was late, anyway. Should he text Katie again? If Akim's accident had been because he stole an eye; and Rasheed felt ill because Samir took the kidney, then…

He checked his phone. Nothing! He tried texting Katie one more time.

Hey! I think something is going on at school with that new teacher, Medon.

As he typed, his phone auto-corrected. It changed *Medon* to *demon*. Samir stared at his phone and a wave of cold came over him.

Chance? Had to be.

So why was he shivering? Again, his heart galloped, seeming to get louder and louder until it filled his bedroom.

Samir climbed back under the covers, shivering, and fell into a deep dreamless sleep.

*

Samir grinned at his reflection in the bathroom mirror and spat his toothpaste out. He'd really let his imagination get the better of him last night! Wait until he told his mates the stupid thoughts he'd had. They'd never let him hear the end of it!

He rinsed and looked into the mirror. His mum was standing behind him. She looked worried.

"Morning. What's wrong, Mum?"

"It's Katie," she put her hand on Samir's shoulder, "she's been taken into hospital."

Samir's spine froze. "What happened?"

"She collapsed at home last night. When she came round she was asking for you. She's fainted before over the past couple of weeks. It's probably nothing. Maybe she just needs extra vitamins. But I thought you should know she won't be in school. Hurry up or you'll be late."

On the bus to school, Samir's mind churned. Third person close to him — third organ he stole! This must have something to do with Mr Medon. *The demon*? He should say something to someone. Even if he sounded crazy, he should mention it. What if someone else got hurt?

Had Medon been telling the truth about the skeleton? Mr Bones had never had that skeleton in class. And it had smelled weird. What if it *had* been a real person? Who could it have been? What if… what if it was Mr Bones, and Mr Medon had murdered him? What if… because Bones had made Medon's life a misery at school, Medon had hunted him down?

What if Medon punished anyone who didn't like him, or who he didn't like?

But, no, that was crazy. Stupid. Samir had just played too many gory video games. There was no proof of anything. The skeleton probably stank because it had been stashed in a musty old attic.

Anyway, if Samir said anything… well, *he* was the one with stolen body parts in his locker, wasn't he? He'd be in trouble.

Maybe this was all his fault.

No. Get a grip. His mum had said Katie had

fainted before. This had nothing to do with him, or that stupid heart he'd stolen!

Samir rushed into school. He headed for his locker and flung it open. Nothing! But he remembered throwing those parts in there. Had he locked the door?

"Looking for something?"

Sweat spread across the back of Samir's neck. His palms were hot and sticky. He rubbed them down the front of his trousers. When he turned round, Mr Medon was grinning, showing his teeth. They were sharply pointed and crowded his mouth, like he had a double, maybe even triple, layer. Samir was hypnotised. Medon surely couldn't close his mouth with all those teeth; they made Samir think of a shark. They were mouldy greeny-yellow all along the gums.

Medon stepped closer, his eyes changed from pale blue into a shimmering, pulsing purple. "You stole from me."

"I'm sorry, Sir. I didn't mean anything—"

"Everything is just a big joke to you. All you think about is yourself."

"I was only messing about," Samir whispered, his voice small.

"Ah yes, hilarious, isn't it? Laughing behind my back," Medon sneered. "Other people can mess around too."

"Sir, have you done something to my friends?" Samir blurted out.

"You ought to be more careful, young man. Actions have consequences. You should know that by now — although perhaps you don't. You're lucky to have any friends, the way that you treat them."

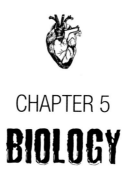

CHAPTER 5
BIOLOGY

Samir turned and ran down the school corridor, towards the doors leading into the playground. He half-expected Mr Medon to chase him but, when he turned to look, the corridor was empty. Where had everyone gone?

The corridor seemed to shift and ripple, and stretch out longer and longer. The overhead strip lights flickered.

He thought he might be dreaming, but he pinched himself and he wasn't asleep! What was happening?

He felt exhausted. He stopped running and put his hands on his thighs. He took deep gulping breaths. Except he couldn't breathe properly. He couldn't get a full breath.

He forced himself on, rushing through the school doors at last, then through the school gates. He didn't care what time it was. He didn't feel well.

His usual bus, the number 66, pulled up at the bus stop. Great! He'd be home soon. He'd be far away from school, and the weird new teacher, and whatever was happening. He'd call his friends and see how they were feeling. Then he'd tell his mum something odd was going on. He would say that maybe his friends had been put under some curse or spell. His mum would know what to do — she always did.

Mum would know what to do.

Get home! Be safe.

The doors of the bus hissed open. Samir stepped on. The bus was full but there was a seat at the front. The driver reminded Samir of Mr Medon, a little. His hair was black and bushy, and he had a big beard, but he was really skinny and there was something strange about his smile. What was that speck of something white in his beard? Samir's eyes widened. It looked like there were maggots crawling around in there!

No. Samir blinked and swallowed hard. His throat was sore. He was just tired and paranoid and maybe coming down with a bug.

"Pass?" The driver grunted.

Samir reached into his back pocket for his bus pass, but it wasn't there.

"Hang on," he said, reaching into his school bag. He dug his fingers down deeper until they touched something cold and round. What was this? He pulled it out. It was the fake eyeball!

Samir dropped it, yelped, and watched it roll
down the bus.

The passengers swivelled their heads. Samir
stared at them. Something was very wrong. Some
passengers didn't have noses. A girl was missing
some fingers; the man next to her had too many.
A woman had a hole in her shoe, and a big toe
oozing green pus poked out of it.

He must be imagining things! Just a bunch of
crazy people getting into Halloween really early.

"I haven't got all day," the driver said.

"Is this your pass?" Samir turned to see who'd
spoken and stared in horror at a man with empty
eye-sockets. The man was holding something out
to him.

Still staring at the eyeless face, Samir held out
his hand. The man put something into it. It was
slimy. It was moving! Samir looked down and
saw a fat, black slug-like creature writhing in his

palm. A leech! "Aaargh!" he yelled and shook the repulsive thing onto the floor.

His tongue seemed to be growing bigger. It swelled and swelled in his mouth until he couldn't swallow. He felt sick. This had to be a nightmare, right? He pinched himself — hard. But no. He was awake.

The driver smiled. "Cat got your tongue?" he cackled. His laugh sliced the air. Samir's eyes were bulging, he was choking.

Then all the passengers started laughing. "We're only joking, Sammy!"

His tongue suddenly shrank to normal size and Samir gasped for air.

He still had one hand deep in his bag. Something wet and slick slapped against his hand and then coiled itself around his wrist. Samir brought his hand out. It was the intestines from Medon's desktop model, but they weren't plastic anymore!